BEHIND THE IRIS

The secret of our eyes

Carlos Patricio Campos A.

Original Title Behind the Iris

ISBN: 9798544442981

Author

Carlos Patricio Campos A.

Country: Chile 2019

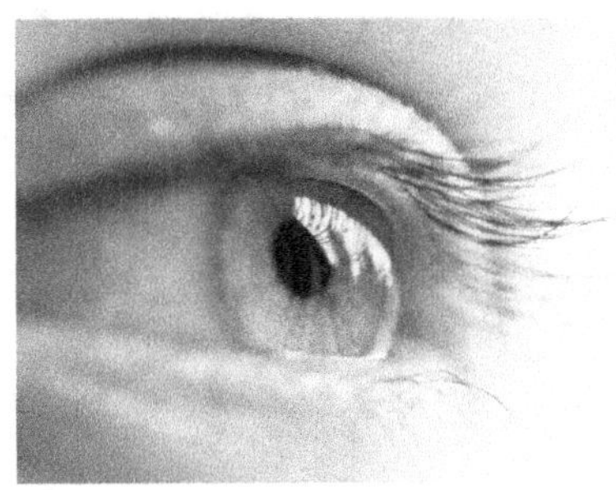

-At the end of the flood, Noah receives a message through the Rainbow.

-Iris is the name given, in Greek Mythology, to the Messenger of God.

-The mystery that had been hidden from ages and ages, has now been made manifest. Col 1:26

-Thou hast made my days a short time, and my age is as nothing before thee. Psalm 39:5

INDEX

INTRODUCTION

Life expectancy is increasing in the world, thanks to advances in technology, science and medicine. On the other hand, viruses and other incurable diseases besiege us and undermine man's efforts to prolong our time on earth by a few more years.

We must recognize then that our stay on this planet is brief and ephemeral.

We are a mist that passes and then dissipates.

Whether we like it or not, we all have our days numbered and, adding and subtracting, they are very few.

Time seems to fly faster and faster and there is so much to do...if only we knew exactly when the clock of life is going to stop. Perhaps then, knowing precisely how much time we have available, we could organize ourselves much better....

Wait! what am I saying?

There is a secret that this story reveals to us.

As we delve into that colorful layer of our eyes, a shocking truth is revealed to us that takes us on an amazing journey with changed lives and clear goals.

Giving us certainties unknown to human beings,

But are we really prepared to face such a shocking truth?

Knowing it can radically change our life...

The Father

Arturo Medina, Henry's father, was born in Puerto Montt. He came to live in Santiago in the 70's after the military coup. He was a fisherman by profession.

In the big city he began working in the central Vega, as a pioneer, helping to load and unload trucks.

Over the years and in contact with the people he discovered an extraordinary gift of discernment that he possessed. He married Cristina, a woman from the capital and they had a son. They named him Henry in honor of Henry Fonda, their favorite actor, and he was born on the same day as their son, May 16.

Gradually Arturo, Henry's father, became known as a clairvoyant, and eventually recognized as the "village healer". He possessed an incredible gift for detecting illnesses in patients who came to visit him.

One of the best known cases was that of an army captain who came to visit him. He was suffering from a strange eye disease called Leber's disease.

The diagnosis of the medical specialists of the military hospital was that he suffered from this disease in sight, and it was incurable. With an accurate and fatal diagnosis that would leave him inexorably blind within a year. When the officer entered Henry's father's office, he said: -You captain suffered an accident when you were young that affected your back, right? - Surprised, he clearly remembered the fall that he suffered the day before presenting himself for the medical examination that would give him the pass to the dream of entering the military career. He never told anyone. The doctors did not detect it and he passed the medical examination well, although the pain in his back was intense for several weeks, until it disappeared.

-Yes, I remember," said the military man, "but what does that have to do with my eyes and my going blind? That was a long time ago.

- Your spine was twisted because of that accident and since then, it has been affecting a nerve that runs through your back. This is what has damaged your eyes

- Henry's father said.

His case was well known since he was accurate in his diagnosis and after a treatment with massages and poultices, the captain, although he did not recover his previous sight, the inexorable advance of his blindness was completely stopped. This allowed the captain to continue with his life in a normal way.

The Mysterious Number

When Henry's father died, all eyes were on his son. Would he have the same gift?

Henry, however, was different and sought his own path. He was a more practical man, restless and very curious and considered himself a researcher. He did not believe in abstract gifts like discernment or clairvoyance.

clairvoyance. "Seeing is believing" he repeated to himself.

He specialized in Iridology or Iriology, an alternative medicine technique that studies the patterns, colors and shades of the iris in patients, in search of a disease.

Henry was an enthusiast; his passion was to study the iris.

Yes, the iris, that muscular, veiled, easily contracted diaphragm in front of the lens of the eye and at the center of which is the pupil!

His research, driven by great curiosity, went beyond the guidelines established by this therapy. This led him to take a course in Statistical Analysis at the University of Chile, which he completed satisfactorily and only lacked the practical part to receive his diploma.

So it was that one day, when he was observing a patient's iris, by chance and for some mysterious reason, he discovered a surprising enigma, a secret inside the human eye. A secret very well kept by nature. Hidden there in the iris, he observed a message, some numbers, to be exact. A hidden number engraved behind the pigmentation of the iris. A kind of number viewer. It appeared there as if it were a Steganography printed between the colors of the eye. At first, Henry thought that perhaps the number he saw there might correspond to the person's age. But after examining several patients, he discovered that this number was permanently engraved and did not change over time. In both a child and an elderly person, these numbers remained unchanged and unique to each individual. A sort of fingerprint hidden there in the eye. In time he was surprised to conclude that this mysterious figure of several numbers represented a sum of days. That it was not the actual age of the person, but the total time of life. Yes, just like that! By reading the iris I could see a multi-digit number. Camouflaged among the colors and shades of the iris. That apparently each

and every one of us has engraved or printed there;
behind the iris.

 After a while he was able to confirm that this
invariable and mysterious figure seemed to be a total
number of days of life. Thus, knowing the date of
birth, Henry could, with a simple subtraction,
determine how long a person had left to live. It
should be noted that this discovery was not made by
studying the DNA or genetic testing of a human
being. Nor by experimenting or manipulating human
embryos, or nanotechnology, or even with a
recognition algorithm. No! It was by studying the
human eye, advanced Iriology, as Henry calls it. He
worked out a kind of chromatic circle where each
color and shade revealed a hidden number. Henry
unknowingly possessed a special gift for visualizing
these numbers in the color spectrum. From an early
age, Henry was known to have privileged eyesight.
He lived for a time with his family in the port of San
Antonio. From the hills he would watch the ships
coming and going with their cargoes enclosed in
containers. Henry was the first to spot a ship
approaching. At first his friends reacted incredulous

at such a statement, until after 5 or more minutes, they also managed to see the approaching ship. At that moment Henry surprised them all again by saying that he could already read the name of the ship, and indeed he could. His friends confirmed it when the ship docked at the port. "Bionic Eye" his companions told him.

 Returning to his discovery, although he shared with other colleagues his finding printed on the iris of patients, none of them could visualize what Henry was able to see. This led him to isolation and scorn from other iriologists. But this did not stop him, he went ahead with his research and tested on several patients. He was able to corroborate that indeed each and every one of us has our own number engraved in the iris. He then postulated that a man's life is expressed in a number of well-defined days. As well defined as the day is followed by night. We know that a day is the time the earth spends to go around itself, equivalent to 24 hours. These days have never varied since man's existence on earth has been known. Therefore, it is an extraordinarily reliable measurement.

The Mother

The first thing he thought of was his grandmother who had recently turned 91 years old, which is equivalent to 32850 days. After doing the study, the result (the figure displayed on her Iris) was 33950 days. In other words, the difference was equivalent to 1100 days; that is, a little more than 3 years of life. His grandmother was happy to have her grandson's undivided attention. -Grandma," Henry told her, "you still have a lot of life ahead of you. She responded with a big smile. However, for Henry and his experiment it was a long time to wait. He then performed the same test on Cristina, his mother who was 54 years old. This time the result was surprising and alarming; she had only 44 days left to live. - 44 days, it can't be! There's something wrong! said Henry. I have to do it again! His mother, who knew him well and saw his frightened face, said, "Don't worry, we'll do it another day. After a few days Henry convinced her to have a medical check-up and routine tests. Everything was normal in his mother's health, but Henry was not at all reassured. He tried several times to convince her to let him examine her iris again. But he could not convince her. His mother finally said to him: son, if you want to see my iris again you must tell me what you saw. How long do I have to live? Henry was silent. "How to reveal such news. I can't say something like that without being absolutely sure," he thought. Finally, he said, "Mom, everything is fine, I just couldn't see the numbers clearly. It's just an experiment, don't worry, let's leave it at that. The days went by too fast and Henry had a funny thing going on, even though he was 30 years old, he felt like a child. He didn't want to leave his mother's side. She had a fast food kiosk and Henry was always willing to help her. In the afternoons she would invite him for a walk and talk about simple things from his childhood while they appreciated the flowers in the neighborhood gardens. Deep in his heart Henry fervently hoped he was wrong. His mother, seeing him so thoughtful, said to him, "Son, please don't feel guilty. You are not the one who decides when someone is going to die. You have a gift to see when it is the end of the road, but you are not the one who decides when and how that end will be. Don't condemn yourself and use that gift for good, leave the rest to God.

That last day, the 44th day, he brought her breakfast in bed. His surprised mother said to him: "Son, what are we celebrating? - Oh mom let me spoil you a little, Henry said.

 During the day he did not leave his mother's side for a minute. At nightfall he went to bed to say goodbye to her. She said a little prayer and Henry finished with a heartfelt amen. He went to his bed and said goodbye to his grandmother. Once in his room he sighed, thinking that he had indeed made a mistake. It was at that moment that he heard his grandmother scream. He ran to his mother's bedside and found her passed out. She was rushed to the nearby hospital, where she arrived deceased. His mother died of a stroke, just before the end of that day. From then on Henry gave up his experiments completely, mourning for a long time, until his grandmother died, 3 years later. He remembered the study he had done on her and it was exactly the 1100 days predicted in his grandmother's iris. "This is much more serious than I had thought," he said to himself. "This is a shocking discovery, both for the person and for his family environment."

 "And while it is an eminent truth, we all have to die, the question is whether we want to know when or not.

There are people who do not want to know, or even think about it. Although we do not want it, the day to leave this world will come.

The Children Leave

He then decided to resume his experiments until he had gathered enough evidence and verified that his discovery was true and could be proven beyond doubt. He moved to the city and managed to get into the clinical hospital, in the children's oncology area. There they accepted him to do his internship; a statistical study of the positive impact of family visits on children's health. Along with that, of course, he developed in secret, what he was most interested in: A study of the exact date of death of several of the little patients.

His experiment was 100% accurate in those children with cancer who died within the 6 months he was there. It was a hard and sad time, seeing those little ones who are only here for a short time and then they are gone. He observed that these little people are like envoys, they live very little time and leave deep teachings in their parents, relatives and friends. He managed to tell a couple of children, in their ears, the date when they would be leaving. They took it with serenity and fortitude. One of them, seeing Henry deeply affected, told him: "Do not grieve, my friend, death is a companion that opens the door to a better world!"

 - All these experiences were too intense for him. Shocked and discouraged, he decided to return to his village and live a quieter life. Then he took over the business his mother had left him. Working there, he tried to forget everything. He no longer wanted to think, talk, or hear about the journey of life that we all make towards the end. So time passed ...

Until one day someone came to see him.

Unexpected Visit

Henry had decided that the secret of his discovery would be buried forever. After all, what good could this do for mankind? Could it make us better people? Humbler? More loving? Could society live with such a resounding truth as that? How could it alter a person's life to know, quite precisely, how many days they have left? Would it be so necessary for medicine to spend huge fortunes on treatments, remedies and clinics when you know the exact date you are going to die? Could science extend the days of life already written in the iris? Too many questions for a mere mortal. "I forget everything and leave it buried where it belongs," he said to himself.

 Thus he was pondering in his thoughts when he was interrupted: Good afternoon! A coffee, please.

- A husky voice said to him. Henry looked up and noticed a young man about 35 years old. He had not

seen him in town before, but his face looked familiar.
-All right, a coffee is on its way out," Henry replied. -
My name is Luis and as you may know I am not from
here. I have come to visit the town and talk to you.

- Very well, tell me," said Henry, pouring the coffee.

-I am a paramedic who works at the hospital where
you did a statistical study last year. Actually, I used to
work there, but now I'm on medical leave. They
discovered a tumor in my brain and the doctors say it
can't be operated on, they gave me 2 to 3 years to
live, he said in a low voice.

- How sorry I am! - said Henry sincerely.

 - What can I do for you?

Lowering his voice even more, the man said to him:

 -I want you to tell me the exact date of my death. I
know you can do that. I'm sorry and I apologize for
getting into your papers when you were there in the
hospital. I swear to you that I have never told anyone
this and I will never tell anyone this. I only ask that
you tell me the day of my death and I will leave in
absolute silence.

Henry was outraged, though more so at himself for having neglected the subject in such a stupid way. He knew he was trapped in a dead end street, as this man could reveal the secret he had decided to bury forever.

-All right, he told him. -But you must promise to keep the secret and take it to the grave.

- I agree! - said Luis. -I promise.

-Tell me your age.

- I am 39 years old," Luis answered.

The number Henry found in Luis' iris was 14140 days. From this number he subtracted the 39 years or 13739 days already lived at the date.

The test´s result was that he had 401 days left to live. That is, 1 year, 1 month and 5 days.
 Luis listened in silence, and shaking Henry's hand he thanked him and asked how much the cost was.
That´s all right, just remember what we promised.
 Luis promised once again that he would keep the secret forever. He went away quietly... it gave him peace to know with certainty the date of his death.

"I'll take it as if I were going on a trip to a distant country" - he thought - "I only have a one-way ticket. I won't need luggage because they will provide me with everything I need there. I have the time for preparations and I must make the most of it."

 The first thing he did was to arrange all the money matters; he sold his house, his car, withdrew the funds from his bank account, distributed his goods among his family and friends and left enough money for the second part: to travel to some places in the world he wanted to visit.

He then arranged and paid for funeral services, his grave, etc. In addition, he wrote a will for his last personal things; his watch that he left to his nephew, the stereo to his sister, his clothes to be donated to people in street situations, etc. Everything well detailed without leaving any loose ends. He also wrote a medical will giving instructions about his last days of life, in which he specified not to be artificially intervened with resuscitation machines, electro shock, artificial respiration, etc. He left his mother in legal charge of defending these decisions.

After he had everything in order, he took advantage of the time to visit some people he had not seen for a long time. He asked for forgiveness and expressed his

love to all his relatives, friends and acquaintances. She reconciled with God, and finally wrote a letter to Henry thanking him for his help.
Seven days before his death he lost consciousness. Then he died quietly and peacefully, the exact date Henry had given him.
 At the funeral, his mother, without realizing what she was doing, read the letter that Luis had left her to give to Henry. She read it aloud to all the attendees, friends and family who listened attentively. This letter recounted, in addition to his thanks, how beneficial it had been that Henry had revealed to him the exact date of his death and how he was able to arrange his departure well. The surprised listeners at the funeral could not believe what Luis' mother was reading. To know exactly the date of his death? Some of them, decided to go the next day to deliver that letter personally and of course to know more of this strange revelation.

The Secret Revealed

The next day Henry awoke early hearing noises and voices outside his house. He looked out the window and saw about 8 or 12 people outside his door. He immediately realized what had happened. These people had found out, through Luis, the secret he had kept. He had no way out and decided to face the situation without hesitation. Henry was aware that it took courage to go and visit him. Not everyone is willing to know such a dramatic truth.

He asked his neighbor Karla to help organize the visitors. And person by person, Henry received them and told them the date of his death.

The first of them, Luis' brother, brought the letter and a generous donation. The others each did the same. There was no commotion. They left quietly. They were all middle-aged people whose death date would be in 20 to 25 years. (Except Ana whose story I will tell you later).

Henry just asked them not to record or write down what he told them. He repeated the result a couple of times so they had to memorize the number he gave them. Outside, on the way out, you would see some of them writing it down on a piece of paper or on their cell phone. Henry didn't want to leave any evidence that someone could use against him. This was something spontaneous and voluntary, under each person's responsibility.

He finished the day exhausted, he had "attended" about 20 people without any problems.

In the evening, he thanked his friend Karla, gave her a tip and said goodbye. Then he took a shower and prepared himself something to eat, when he heard a knock on his door.

-It's locked! - he shouted in annoyance.

- I'm just here to deliver a package! I need you to sign for it and I'll leave you alone!

-. Impatiently he opened the door and found himself facing a man with a gun pointed at him. The man looked agitated and nervous.

- Let me in! - he said, pushing Henry violently. He closed the door and forced him to sit down.

- Let me be clear, I want you to tell me the date of my death right now! The doctors say that because of the advanced cancer I have, I only have a couple of years. I want you to stop lying to me and tell me exactly when I'm going to die.

- Okay, that's fine! - Henry said. -Put the gun away, you don't have to point it at me all the time.

- The result was not at all encouraging. Before telling
him he asked him if he was really sure he wanted to
know.
The man raised his pistol again and staring at him
said:
- Don't lie to me, say it now! -

-You will die in 27 days. - said Henry.

The man's eyes bugged out, he turned the table over
and with a violent blow knocked Henry to the
ground. The man went out into the street where
several neighbors had gathered and, hearing the
screams, had called the police who were already
approaching with sirens blaring.

The man shouted madly: "This man is a fake, he says I
will die in 27 days, but I won't! - It won't be like that!
And putting the pistol to his mouth he shot himself
there in front of everyone, falling heavily to the
ground.

The commotion caused shook the whole town. The
man was taken in agony to the hospital. Henry was
arrested and spent the night at the town police
station.

The Judge

The next day he was brought before the Judge who received him in his chambers.

-Tell me, what do you really do? Remember, this is confidential, no one will know what we talk about here. But tell me the truth. Are you some kind of prophet?

- Henry smiled, raised his head and said:

- Nothing like that, it's just a study of the iris that I do on the person, and with it I can tell how much longer he will live.

- Ah, that's a good way of looking at it! - said the Judge.

-But it scares the person, it worries them, it takes them out of their daily life! It's a very difficult thing to handle and? it can drive you crazy like the man who attacked you yesterday!

Yes - said Henry, - but so far that was the only violent case. What I tell people is a truth that anyone who wants it, can know. Humans are like yogurts; we have the expiration date marked. I can read that date and tell them.

- I understand, - but tell me, - what happens to a person who knows the date of his death and decides to end his life? Or does he die in an accident?

-I don't know," Henry replied, "this discovery is something new and I don't know yet the consequences of revealing something so dramatic and that has remained a secret for thousands of years. There are many questions and consequences that are still unknown and unsuspected by mankind.

I do not know how a person will die, whether by natural causes, disease or accident.

It seems to me that the only option to alter that date would be suicide. But it could also be," Henry continued, "that the person, knowing exactly how long he or she has left to live, would be encouraged to desist from such a tragic decision.

- This all sounds very interesting, but why do you do it? - asked the magistrate.

-I think, said Henry, -that the person, knowing the date of his death, will have his priorities clearer and will be able to organize his life better.

Knowing the exact date of his departure, he will feel how short life is and perhaps he will not waste his time looking for big material dreams in the long run, even extensive and expensive medical treatments that do not always help.

- So, are you saying that we should not take care of ourselves or go to the doctor when we are sick?

- No, that's not it," Henry continued, "what I'm saying is that we should take care of ourselves as much as we can.

 The goal is to live as well as possible with a good quality of life, for as long as God wants us to.

When the time comes for us to pass on to the next world, I am sure we will all want to do so with the peace of mind that we took good care of our bodies, to the best of our ability. And if we have not been doing so, we need to start today.

However, we all know that no matter how well we take care of ourselves, we are all, of course, going to die. Therefore, we must be aware of how brief our time on earth is.

We can make plans for the future and prepare for it with the time we have, but without fear or worry since the end will come anyway.

Why worry if one cannot and will not be able to add a single day, not even an hour more to one's existence?

My wish is that the person, knowing the number of days left, will feel more clearly the importance of living with love. Then the person will be more dedicated to live and not only to survive.

He will not put off that project or dream for later, if he knows how little time he has left.

Just like the example of yogurts, when the expiration date is approaching, they are placed ahead to be sold, - people will have a different, more compelling and positive outlook on life," - Henry concluded.

-One more question," added the Judge.

Surely you don't know, but in your opinion, is it possible to increase the days of life already recorded in the iris?

-I don't think so- replied Henry -I haven't seen it happen so far.

-All right- said the judge -I have another question.

-Are you the only one who knows how to read the iris this way?

Do you know of anyone else, past or present, who does something like this?

-I really don't know- said Henry.

-It is possible that there are more people with this gift today somewhere in the world.

-I know of a Christian group called the Cathars. They existed in the Middle Ages and lived outside the influence of the Catholic Church. Legend says that among them there were people who possessed this gift and could read the Iris in this way.

The Cathars were brutally exterminated, but they left written that they would return at the end of time with a final message. -said Henry.

And what is that message? - asked the Judge.

-I don't know yet, answered Henry.

 -Do you consider yourself a Cathar? asked the Judge

-In part yes, since I am a Christian, but I do not belong to any religion or church. - answered Henry with a smile.

-That's fine, said the Judge, -but you must be careful, this could be detrimental to many. There are economic groups that will not like it, insurance brokers, banks etc.

-This could bring a big commotion and that would not be easy to handle. Be very careful, keep it low profile.

-Finally, since there are no charges against you, I must let you go free.

One last question - can you do the study with only one photograph?

- I don't know; I haven't tried it. Henry sai

- Please do! -the judge told him-, passing him a photograph of him. -Send me the result by email. On the back I wrote down my date of birth and my email address.

The judge immediately released him. Henry left through a side door, dodging the press, and went to a hostel.

From there he called his neighbor friend, Karla, asking her to come into his house and bring him his things. He asked her to do it discreetly as there were people waiting for him to return. He gave her a list of things to bring: the money, his notebook and clothes. He would wait for her in the afternoon at a certain point.

Later when he met her friend, he thanked her for the favor and asked her not to say anything to anyone. She hugged him and wished him luck.

Days later it was learned that the man who had attacked him and subsequently shot himself, agonized for 26 days. On the 27th he finally died.

Ana

Ana was studying medicine at the University of Chile. Her father, a respected and internationally recognized physician, instilled in her as a child to follow in his footsteps.

She had met Luis at the hospital and upon learning of his death, she attended the funeral where she also heard the reading of the letter sent to Henry. So she decides, like everyone else, to visit him that afternoon. She is accompanied by her boyfriend Ignacio, also a second year medical student.

Ana is in her first year and invites Ignacio, who unwillingly accompanies her.

Both had promised not to say anything, no matter what happened in that meeting with Henry.

To Ignacio it all sounded more like a game than something to be taken seriously.

Already in front of Henry, he asks them why they want to know how long they will live if they are still so young.

-Well, says Ignacio in a superficial tone, -as young brides and grooms we want to project ourselves and achieve the goals we have set for ourselves.

Ana keeps silent. She has a feeling and doesn't want to say anything.

-Okay, says Henry, -let's start with Ignacio.

-No, I'm just here to accompany Ana. I don't want to know those things. That's something I couldn´t get out of my head, I'd rather ignore it.

-Well, says Henry, -then it's only Ana.

Let's see, the number is... 10220 days and you have 19 years which equals 6935 days lived. 3285 days left or 9 years of life.

- Nine years, are you sure? - Ignacio exclaims in surprise.

Ana stands up, shakes Henry's hand and says:

- thank you very much, I appreciate it! And she leaves. In the car on the way home, Ignacio says to her;

-You're not going to take seriously what that madman has told you. You know, that's insane, nobody can know how long a person is going to live.

He can't prove it! There's no scientific evidence!

It's really crazy! You can't make decisions based on an unfounded prognosis!

- A tear escapes Ana and she says:

- I can't ignore or overlook news like this! I hope it doesn't work out just as Henry has said and I live for many more years!

But it's up to me to come to terms with this revelation and make decisions according to this reality!

- But my love, we had so many beautiful plans together! - exclaims Ignacio.

Exactly! - We had plans, you said so! And although it hurts my soul to leave you, our relationship ends today!

You surely have a long life ahead of you! Be happy, live with passion and if you can, keep me in a corner of your heart!

- Wait! - Ignacio says - You can't be serious! We can't end so suddenly!

- Tell me - says Ana, looking into his eyes.

If the news of living only a few more years had come to you, what would you do?

- Well, says Ignacio, hesitating, -I don't know! Maybe I would continue studying and die with the satisfaction of being a doctor, even if I only managed to practice for a year or two.

- Exactly! - says Ana, -I still have 6 or 7 years of studies left, not counting 3 or 4 years of specialty. I don't have time to become a doctor and for me that is no longer important. We are very different Ignacio. I want my life to have a deeper value.

- The truth, she continued, -is that I consider it a privilege to know precisely how much time I have left to live, since we are not aware of the brevity of life. Most of us think we have more time than we actually do. We are rarely ready for the end to come. You have your life and you must live it as you see fit. I will live according to this new way of looking at life and may it be what God wills.

- Then she said goodbye and got out of Ignacio's car and entered her house. Her father and mother had been waiting for her for a while.

- Hello my love, how nice that you arrived! Your father has a surprise for you. Come down as soon as you can, we want to talk to you. Dinner is ready.

- Yes mom! I'll be right down. - Ana answered.

After a while she came down to sit at the table next to them. Her heart was racing, she felt anxious and nervous about this meeting with her parents.

Although she had not clear the whole picture, there was a light shining in the bottom of her heart as if showing her the way forward.

- Dad, she said, -I want to tell you something important.

- Wait, her mother interrupted, -let your father give you the surprise he has prepared for you.

- Here, daughter! - said her father with a big smile, - You've earned it!

You've earned it! You passed your first year of college with flying colors, that's why these keys to your new car are yours!

- But Dad, said Ana.

- Don't say anything, it's yours, you've earned it! Now enjoy it! Why don't you eat and then go see it! - said her mother. - It's in the garage and tomorrow you can go out in it! - completed his father enthusiastically.

-This is not going to be easy - thought Ana, - if I don't say it now it will be harder and harder.

- Finally, taking a deep breath, she said, -Thank you very much dad! I thank you from the bottom of my heart, but I want to be honest with you!

-What I'm going to tell you I know it's going to hurt you a lot!

But I trust that you will understand me, if not now, then in time you will understand!

- Father, she tells him. - I'm making a very important decision in my life! I know you won't like it, but I will listen to my heart!

I know you've always wanted to see me as a recognized and successful doctor like you dad! But life is so short that I've definitely decided to quit my studies!

What I want and actually have always wanted to do, you know, is a job that helps others!

- But daughter! - interrupted her father, "Being a doctor is the best way to help people!

- Dad, continued Ana, -let me explain.

-What people need most, in these difficult times we live in, is someone who shows them by example that you care about them and that you really love them! People need to have their souls healed, to be listened to and to feel that they have an unconditional friend! With medicine I can perhaps do some good, but I believe that what people need most is love, and I have plenty of that-.

- I can't believe what I'm hearing right now, says the father, -What do you mean, leave the career? For how long? Will you take a sabbatical?

- I don't know yet, Dad.

But what does your boyfriend Ignacio say," asks her mother.

-We are finished, answers Ana.

- Oh God, this is crazy, daughter!

-A few days later, with calmer spirits. her father tells her:

-That's fine, daughter, you can take a year off and take the opportunity to travel and get to know other countries. I'm sure you'll come back to your career with more enthusiasm. -

Ana travels to Africa where she comes into contact with a Christian mission in Niamey, the capital of

Niger, and loves to work as a volunteer there. Without realizing it, in that children's home, her life takes on a different meaning, she is busy all day long, she arrives tired to sleep, but happy. She stays there for several years. She has found her life's vocation.

Later, she and an African friend founded a mission in Mozambique. After a few years, her parents visit her and are proud of the work their daughter is doing there.

The government of Mozambique gives her a public recognition and in her speech of thanks she says: - Thanks to all those who have supported me, my parents, colleagues and friends. Especially to Henry who bravely told me a truth that changed my life forever.

Anne died in an accident at the age of 28, the exact date Henry had given her.

"I am only to pass through this world once. Whatever good I can do, whatever gesture of kindness I can show to a human being, help me to do it now and not put it off, for I will never pass this way again."
Stevens Grell

Diego Enrique

In the hostel room, Henry thought about what step to take, in what direction and what to do next. He didn't want a lot of publicity, he knew that this thing he was doing was very delicate and dangerous. One idea that was going around in his head was to go to another country... He was thinking about it when suddenly his phone rang, waking him up.

It was the judge. - Please! - he said in a hurried voice.

- I have a friend who needs to see you urgently! I told him about you and he asked me to come and see him. You are a kind of lifeline for him. Please go and visit him. I'd appreciate it a lot! -

- Okay, okay, okay! -Henry replied, -Give me the person's information.

-His name is Diego Enrique. Don't worry about how to get to his house. He will send a car to pick you up.

Give me your address and he will be by in half an hour.

After a while they came to pick him up. The car took him through the center of the city and then drove away to a well-to-do residential area, where it stopped in front of some white columns and a large wrought iron gate, painted black. It opened at that instant and they entered, closing immediately behind them.

Then the car continued along a white, undulating road, surrounded by trees and gardens with different colored flowers until they reached an English-style mansion.

The chauffeur stopped the car and opened the door for Henry, smiling. He guided him to the door where a distinguished-looking, white-haired man of about 65 was waiting for him.

-Hello, good afternoon. My name is Diego Enrique. My friend spoke very well of you. Please come in.

-Thank you. My name is Henry; how do you do? How can I be of service? I see that you have a very good economic situation, your house is very nice.

-Yes," said Diego Enrique, but the truth is that I am alone, my wife and my two children died in a car accident a month ago. They left from one moment to the next, without warning, without saying goodbye," he said sadly.

-I'm so sorry, Henry replied.

-I'll be honest with you, said the man.

-The sadness is deep and painful, we had planned so many things together, and now I don't know what to do. I must confess that I tried to commit suicide. The driver saved me and prevented me from achieving that macabre goal.

I told my friend the Judge about it last week. He told me about you and your strange gift and I would like you to tell me more.

-Well, said Henry, -what I can do is read the iris in your eyes and determine how many days of life you have ahead of you.

-Unbelievable," said Diego Henry, "You mean I can find out today how much time I have left to meet

Ester, my beloved wife, Macarena and Albertito, my beloved children?

-Yes, answered Henry.

-This is amazing, please let's do it right away.

-Okay, give me your date of birth:

07/11/1953 -until today you have lived 24108 days that is 66 years. In your iris I can read 25308 days. Then you have 1200 days left to live or 3 years, 3 months and 15 days," said Henry.

Diego Enrique was silent for a long time, looking out the windows until he finally reacted:

-Well, that's good news. I thought it might be a much longer wait. Twelve hundred days will go by flying. I have a lot to do to get ready to leave on that date. Do you have any advice for me, dear Henry?

-No, my friend," said Henry, I imagine your head is racing at the moment. I'm sure you know better than anyone what to do with your life. -

-Yes, you're right, said Diego Enrique.

-At first I was a little sad that I wasn't leaving today or tomorrow, but on second thought, I don´t feel ready to meet my family for now.

I hope to learn everything important in this short time I have left on this earth and be ready for that day when I will be able to embrace them with all my love.

-Well Henry, how much do I owe you? -

-Nothing, said Henry.

- Of course you do, answered Diego Enrique, "here is a check, a contribution to your beautiful work.

The driver will take you back wherever you want and if you need anything, anything at all, call me and I'll be happy to help you....

He hugged him, and thanking him once again, they said goodbye.

Henry got into the car and drove away quietly, looking out the window. The sky was starry and the moon was shining, covering the night with light.

One more day of life, he said to himself.

The Train

Back at his hotel early in the morning, Henry finally decided to travel south. He made his way to the railroad station where he bought a ticket to the farthest town, and immediately blended in with the crowd of passengers.

His ticket was H36. He looked for car H and got on. He walked down the aisle until he found seat 36. Directly in front of his seat was a young woman, about his age, with a child who appeared to be her son. As he was putting on his backpack, Henry noticed that the boy was saying something in her ear and she was smiling.

As they sat across from each other, their eyes met. Henry reached out his hand to the boy and said, "Hi, how are you? The boy looked at his mother and she smiled and said, -Say hello to the gentleman!

 The boy shook her hand without saying anything.

- How do you do, young man!, Then he stretched out his hand to her saying.

-My name is Henry.

She shook his hand smiling,

-How do you do, I'm Monica and this is my son Mike.

"What a bright smile", Henry thought to himself.

The train started moving, -Train south! said Henry in an amused tone.

- Yes, she said, -where are you going?

- Actually, I don't know yet, he said half embarrassed, but immediately he asked him another question,

-And where are you going?

- To Los Angeles, she said.-I live and work there.

At that moment the boy tugged his mother's sleeve and whispered something in her ear that made her smile.

- Do you need anything? - asked Henry.

- No, nothing! she said, -the truth is that my son has a kind of gift, that by looking at a person he can see some things that we don't normally see.

- How interesting! - said Henry trying to hide his surprise.

-He says you have a very big secret of your own. I told him we all have some secrets. So don't worry.

 -Do you believe in these special gifts?

- Yes, my father had a wonderful gift that allowed him to see sickness in a person just by looking at them, Henry replied, - Your son seems to be very special!

-We just came from the hospital, she said.

 -It was the last chemotherapy session and we hope it really is the last. Mike was very sick, but he is doing much better now. God willing, he will get better.

-Yes," said Henry, "I'm sure it will be all right.

The train was moving fast and through the window we could see the houses, streets and country scenery. The sun was already moving away towards the sea....

-I can also say that I have a kind of gift, she said suddenly.

- Is that so? said Henry interested.

 - Yes, I often have very vivid dreams. Some have come true over time, some have not. Some repeat themselves, others I don't understand. But I'm always dreaming, she finished with a smile.

- Let's see, tell me one that repeats itself and I don't understand it. Maybe together we can find a meaning for it, said Henry.

-Okay, I'll tell you one that has been repeated lately: I'm crossing a very narrow bridge. It's a bridge for people only. In the distance a man approaches; he looks quiet but mysterious. When he arrives right in front of me he stops and says: I want to show you something. Immediately he opens his shirt and on his chest, as if embedded, there is a huge watch. It is at that moment that I always wake up, frightened.

Henry was stunned, speechless!

Questions came quickly to his mind;

How could a perfect stranger dream about him?

Because without a doubt, the man in the watch was him, as he described him perfectly.

After a few seconds in silence, he finally throws himself into the void and decides to tell her the whole truth.

-You may say, he began, Henry, -that I too have a gift. But before I explain to you what it is, I will tell you that the man with the watch looks a lot like me, and I will tell you why.

He then told him his story, his discovery. The rejection of his fellow Iriologists, his experience with his grandmother, with his mother, at the children's hospital, at home and in front of the judge.

And continued -Iriology claims that the patterns, colors and shades of the iris in the eye, as interpreted by scholars, can detect disease. I for some mysterious reason, which I cannot explain, can see a hidden number behind each color and shade.

For example, a light brown color, when I look at it carefully, I discover a number 2. Then, in the next color or shade I discover another number, 5 for example. So on and so forth until a maximum number of 5 digits is reached. For example, 25500.

-For a long time I didn't know what that number referred to. Until I literally realized that this number indicates a total of days.

 At first I thought it was some kind of mark indicating a person's age, like trees! You know, the circles on their trunk that represent the years lived. But it wasn't that!

Surprised I discovered that each of us has registered, hidden in the iris, the total number of days we will live in this body. And the amazing thing is that I can read it!

- Amazing! said Monica, excited.

- Look! continued Henry, -if we convert the 25500 days from the previous example, it gives us a total of 70 years. If we take away from this number the number of days since birth, we get the exact date of how many days that person has left to live.

- Incredible and fabulous! she said,

- Mom! said the boy interrupting as he tugged on his mother's arm. She leaned over and he said something in her ear.

-Yes! Let's ask him! she said aloud.

-Mike wants to know how many days he has left to live? Could you please help us?

-Ok said Henry, but aren't you afraid to know something so delicate?

- No, not at all! We know how beautiful it is what awaits us there, said Monica whith conviction.

There was she smile again, "I really like her", thought Henry

- That's all right! said Henry, hiding his feelings.

After a while the result to the boy was 10950 days, or 30 years. You've lived 12! You still have 18 more long years to live champion!

- Yes! This means that my son is cured! said the mother. And they both applauded excitedly and Monica hugged Mike and then Henry.

He was also excited and felt joy for the boy and love for her. Yes, it could only be love, how else could he describe that sweet feeling that welled up in him. They stared into each other's eyes, for several seconds. Monica was excited and delighted with him.

- Are you peering into my iris? she said jokingly.

Henry laughed, -No, I'm just looking at your inner beauty. You know what they say; the eyes are the windows to the soul.

-But tell me, where does this tranquility and joy in facing a truth like this come from? Henry asked.

-Ah, that's no secret, she said -I firmly believe there is another life after this one. I also believe that He planned in advance the days of our life, choosing the exact time of your birth, as well as the time of your death.

Here we are just passing through, like the story of the tourist who came to a shepherd's hut and saw that he was living with very little furniture. So he asked him why he had no more furniture. The shepherd replied: I don't see that you come with much luggage either.

Well, said the young tourist, "I'm just passing through.

Ah! said the pastor, so am I!

-Excellent story, said Henry smiling.

-Yes, continued Monica, -when you talk about dying, you have to turn to an expert, someone who knows about death, someone who has been through it and came out of it with flying colors, right? Well, this God-Man, that humble carpenter from Nazareth, spoke that there is another life after this one and that He would prepare a place for us.

If we believe in an afterlife, the goal of each day should be to prepare us for our final day.

Whether or not we have used this time well will be seen at the next level.

Actually, what you tell us with your study, is the day when we pass the course. It is the date, when our practice ends and we pass to the next level.

Therefore, it should not be a date of sadness but of joy. Of course, it hurts to leave your family and friends, and you have to live a mourning, but the separation is only for a while like someone who goes on a trip, then we will all meet again.

That's the wonderful thing about your discovery, knowing the exact date of our death, forces us to realize how imminent and real it is. Monica finished saying.

-I have a question that I will take the opportunity to ask you Monica, said Henry.

- Do you think that the number that I see in the iris, which indicates the total number of days of a person's life, can it be increased?

-I don't think so, said Monica,

-As I said before, each of us is a unique creation of God with a specific time on earth. Both on the day of his birth and the day of his death. However, as every rule has its exception; the Bible in 2Kings chapter 20 tells this story:

"In those days Hezekiah fell sick unto death. And Isaiah the prophet came to him, and said unto him, thus saith the Lord, set thine house in order: for thou shalt die, and not live. And the king repented, and prayed, and wept many tears... and God said unto him, I have heard thy prayer, and seen thy tears: behold, I will heal thee; and I will add unto thy days fifteen years, even 5475 days more. And he did so.

- How interesting and you are absolutely right, although for many people, continued Henry,

-it can be frightening and according to what the judge told me it can also be dangerous. Many can profit from this and take advantage of it by having privileged information, to profit from it. That is why I have to look for a safe place where I can help people on a voluntary basis.

- I'll tell you what, Monica said without taking her eyes off him, -you can come with us to Los Angeles, the city where I live. You stay in an inn and then I'll help you find a better place.

- I'd love to! Henry said enthusiastically.

-I know the city, I was born and raised there. I have my car at the station and I'll take you to a good inn I know, she added.

The train was now pulling into the Los Angeles station. The noise of its heavy wheels screeched, as the engineer applied the brakes and the engine's whistle broke the silence of the falling night.

As the city lights began to twinkle, they climbed down together, Monica, Mike and Henry walked to the car.

Arriving at the Inn, she stopped the car and Henry said a grateful goodbye, telling her:

-it was a wonderful trip, I'm sure it was God who put you on my path. I already have your phone number, so I will call you tomorrow, he said finally.

-I'll wait for you here, go and see if there is room. Monica told him. She left the engine running and as Henry drove away. Mike her son said to her:

- Mom, I like him, I like him too, she replied enthusiastically. Five minutes later Henry came back. - -There is no room here. But they pointed me to a boarding house down the street.

- Okay, let's go, I'll take you there! said Monica. On the way she added;

- I know that pension and it's not the best. I propose you something better. If you don't mind sleeping on a big sofa I have at home, and you accept a hot soup. You can come with us. It's almost dark and...

I gladly and gratefully accept! interrupted Henry.

A Team

Back home after a nice informal and relaxed dinner, she went with her son Mike to help him to bed.

-If you want to take a bath, here it is and there are towels,

- Thank you so much! It will do me a lot of good. Henry thanked her.

After the bath he went to the living room that would be his bedroom, after a while Monica came with some blankets and sheets, as she approached Henry got up from the couch,

-I'll help you, said Henry, taking the blankets and casually touching her hands, looking into each other's eyes they got closer. Both could feel each other's heart beating, they melted into a short kiss, like tasting ice cream, then a longer, deeper and tighter kiss.

They both laughed as they stumbled over the blankets on their feet.

-Let's make your bed,said Monica, stepping back.

- That's fine, replied Henry.

It was love at first sight, and there on that sofa a passionate love was consummated. A happy encounter between two beings who unknowingly sought each other for a long time, wandering in a world of strangers.

Henry was overflowing with happiness, and so was she. They looked like children again, feeling something pure, selfless and sincere in their hearts.

The next day as they ate breakfast in the kitchen with Mike, Monica said, -I had a dream last night.

- Tell it! said Henry and Mike in unison.

-The three of us were on a sandy beach, running from a swarm of wasps and escaping into the sea.

-That's right, I thought of that, said Henry,

-We should prepare for an eventual chase. You never know who might be interested in the secret I have discovered.

- But you are safe here, said Monica,

- Yes, thank you, said Henry, giving her a kiss on the forehead,

-Anyway, let's plan an escape in case of emergency. We must have a shelter to escape to and live for a while without having to come back here.

- Yes, said Mike, -it could be a cabin in the mountain range, -good idea, they both said, -let's go for a walk and look for something like that.

-Yes, and it has to be today, since I work tomorrow and young Mike has to go back to school. Monica added.

They headed towards the mountain range, to the heights of the Biobío river, a generous river that runs undulating, joyful and crosses Chile from the mountains to the sea.

There in the mountain range and near some hot springs of warm and crystalline waters, they found and rented a cabin for 3 months. They told the lady who owned the cabins that Henry was a writer and they would come from time to time to spend a few days, to keep the cabin always ready.

 Henry changed his appearance, he always wore a beard, this time he shaved it off and started wearing a pair of glasses. The key word was "wasps", if mentioned it was a serious emergency and they were to go to that cabin and meet there.

During the week Henry traveled there alone, carrying supplies and everything they needed to spend a season without lacking anything. He stayed there for a few days and returned to Monica's house.

She was his joy in life, he had fallen deeply in love with this beautiful woman. Monica also reciprocated his deep love for him.

They quickly learned to share their hearts, to speak with sincerity and understanding, and their friendship grew day by day. Henry helped in any way he could, shopping and doing household repairs. Mike often accompanied him and they got along well.

A happy family had been formed again. Something that had been broken when their father abandoned them many years before.

The Wasps

-Here is the report Mr. Smith. Ok let me see the press release first. "Man dies after agonizing 27 days, the exact day predicted by Henry."

-What do we know about this Mr. Henry?

-Henry Medina, is Chilean, lives in El Monte, a small town near Santiago. According to our preliminary investigation, he has a particular gift that allows him to determine the day of a person's death through his eyes.

- What certainty is there in all this? - So far, sir, in our research there are at least 3 real cases with 100% effectiveness.

-Ok, through our consulate in Chile, I commissioned a team to locate this man and find out everything related to this gift he claims to have. If indeed the discovery made by this Mr. Henry is real, we must have him here.

This is a job for the CIA and it will mean a well-prepared plan to avoid getting into trouble with the Chilean justice system. The first thing is to discredit this man, any attempt of veracity we must fight it with denials and witnesses who say that everything is false.

Once we achieve this objective, we propose support and support and we bring him "voluntarily" here, in security so that he can carry out his studies.

-If he leaves the country, arrest him at the first airport he arrives at, with an accusation of attempted rape of an American citizen. - Yes, sir! -

The agents arrived at Henry's former neighbor Carla. She denied knowing anything about him. Although through her cell phone the agents obtained the last conversation she had with him.

She didn't know where he was staying, but after a few days they found out the hostel where he stayed.

 There they lost track of him until they checked the cameras at the bus and train terminals and managed to see him boarding a train to the south.

They still had to find out which city he was heading to. For weeks they checked the cameras at each station until they saw him getting off at the Los Angeles station with a woman and a child. Enlarging the photo, they identified the woman, Monica Ubilla, and her son Mike. This gave them his home and work address.

The next day they were already in the city, a woman showed up at Monica's house. She was not there; she had gone out with Henry to the supermarket.

Mike opened the door and she showed up offering a new TV plan. Mike told her that his mom was out. They left him a brochure with the TV offer. They also gave him a beautiful pencil as a gift.

-Thank you, Mike said and closed the door.

He already knew what to do; he took his cell phone and sent his mother a message with only one word "Wasps".

-Relax, said Henry to Monica as she became alarmed at the message,

-you go home in a cab, I'll take the car and I'll let you know when to come get it, right here. I will go to the cabin. Don't call or text me. I will contact you when I find a safe way.

Giving him a kiss they parted, not knowing what would happen with their future.

At the cabin

From the cabin Henry went for a walk in the surroundings. The forests invited to relax and the pure air of the pre mountain range revitalized the energies. After a while walking, he met some muleteers who were taking their animals to the top of the summit in search of green pastures for their food.

- Where is our friend going? asked Henry,

- Ah, we still have a long way to go, said the man who seemed to be the most experienced,

-We are very close to the border with Argentina, he added.

- Can we get there on foot? Henry asked more and more interested.

-No, said the man, it has to be on horseback and even then it is difficult. It is about 5 hours from here.

- Thank you, said Henry, -Have a good trip!

He stood there watching them ride away up the mountain range. He already had a clearer idea of where he could flee to.

On his way back to his cabin, he asked where he could rent horses.

The next day he went in search of the Pincheira family who had horses.

- Do you have horses to lease? I would like to ride to the border. -said Henry.

The lady replied: -I am going to be honest with you. I can rent you horses, but you have to go with my oldest son, he knows the region well and can serve as a guide. You will have to pay for his services.

- All right, said Henry. -I will let you know in a few days; I would like to take my family so I will let you know when we are ready.

In the meantime, Monica returned home and her son was waiting nervously to tell her about the visit he had had from the supposed promoter of television services. He showed her the pencil he had been given. Monica examined it carefully and discovered a small microphone. So she immediately proceeded to throw it away.

-Well done, Mike, for letting us know in time, she said.

- Now don't worry, there's nothing to be afraid of, our job is to throw these people off the scent.

They don't know that we are aware of their presence, so we'll act naturally.

The next day she took her son to school and went to work.

When she arrived, her boss called her into his office. There was a woman and a man waiting for her.

-Sit down, we just want to ask you a few questions.

-Do you know this man?

 They showed her a picture of Henry with a beard and without glasses.

Monica hesitated a little and finally said.

-He looks like a man who approached me on the train and he asked me how to go to Angol, a nearby city. I told him where the bus terminal to that city was.

- Did he tell you anything else? - Not really, no. I just gave him that information. Why are you looking for him?

-That's none of your business, they said,

-but if you see him you must give me the information right away at this phone. The man is very dangerous. Any help you give him will be considered an accomplice. Take care of your work and family and stay out of trouble, they finally told her.

Meanwhile, another team was questionning the people who had been examined by Henry looking for inconsistencies and errors. They interviewed other iriologists who did not believe in Henry's supposed theories. Then they contacted some newspapers to publish denials and interviews denying the veracity of Henry's postulations.

The smear plan was underway. All that remained was to locate this Henry.

Roberto

Meanwhile Henry was holed up in his cabin waiting for the next move to be made. He was doing just that when he received a visit from the lady who rented horses.

-Good afternoon, she said. -Sorry to bother you, but it is something very important and I want to ask for your help.

- Tell me, said Henry, surprised.

-It's about my son, he is in a very bad way, he has a tremendous depression and I don't know what to do to help him. He doesn't want to see a doctor and I think that if you talk to him you could help him in some way. I told him that you want to lease horses and that gives me the ideal excuse to come and talk to you. Please could you help him?

-All right, said Henry, -don't worry, I'll do my best.

After lunch, Roberto was already there, he was coming to know details of the leasing of his horses.

He quickly empathized with the young man. Little by little the conversation flowed and Henry finally told him;

-You know Roberto; I have a big secret to tell you: by studying people's eyes I can tell how long they have left to live on this earth.

Roberto opened his eyes in surprise, -But how can that be?

-It seems we all have our days numbered, said Henry, even if we don't know it. I figured out how to discover the exact days we have left to live.

- Ah, how interesting! But what if someone decides to shorten those days? said Roberto.

-If you mean a suicide, in that case I guess you would arrive earlier than planned to the place that was prepared for you and miss several things, as well as the welcome party.

I will tell you a story to explain it:

-Once upon a time I received well in advance an invitation to a celebration party, where I would receive an award for having been a good companion. All my friends and former classmates would be there, as well as my parents, aunts, uncles and cousins. Everyone was invited.

The place was at the big event hall in town. They would have a live band and lots of good food and drinks.

On the invitation card, it said my name, the place and the date; October 21 of that year.   But I was so excited about the idea of attending that party, that I read without realizing it, August 21. That means, 2 months before the celebration.

Arriving on that August 21, I put on my best shirt, a tie and my favorite suit and with my shoes shining, I headed to the large village hall. It was raining that afternoon.

When I arrived at the event hall, the first thing that caught my attention was how unkempt the garden was.

The gate was closed, so I slipped through a hole in the fence. There was no music to be heard either, it was eerily quiet. As I entered the ballroom, the floor was broken, you could tell everything was under construction. There was no light and no people. I got cold and felt lonely and sad.

Then I saw a poster of the party on the wall and realized my mistake.

I had arrived two months before the appointed date!

This seems to be very similar to what happens when someone commits suicide. By arriving earlier, your family, friends and those who love you and are already there, will also be saddened by not being able to receive you as they wanted. There would be no party, celebration or gifts. None of that.

Only a deep sadness of those who were left here.

I know a mother, who never spoke again, because of the grief she suffered, when she learned that her son had committed suicide.

 Roberto lowered his gaze and remained silent, then said sadly:

-Maybe I don't want to party. -

- Of course you do! said Henry.

- Let's be honest, we all want to feel loved, we all want to be happy in this life and even more so in the next life. If we don't manage to be happy here, our wish is that in the next life, we will be happy.

Here we are only passing through, we have a few days to live and they pass very quickly. Life of course is not easy and sometimes it is hard to reach the end of each day. Problems can overwhelm us, negative thoughts discourage us, people's selfish actions make us angry, etc.

Then darkness looms over our head, advertising and glossy commercials with their short phrases like "You can do it", "Just Do It", sound to you like an invitation to commit suicide. "It's easy, quick and short."

 But if you have a little patience and hang in there for one more day, you'll see that every morning is a new day. What I do is that I forget what happened yesterday and at dawn I am renewed by the fresh air, the sunrise. I say to myself, today I will learn something new, today I want to be a better person, maybe I will make a new friend.

Like you, my friend Roberto! I am glad to meet you!

The young man smiled, -I'm glad too, he said cheerfully.

 - Listen at the following, continued Henry,

- The number that each of us has inscribed on our irises is a total of days. Not years, months, hours or minutes. It is expressed in days and in reality life is lived in days. You can only deal with one day at a time.

God created the world in 6 days, I don't believe that it took him thousands of years to do it. If God is God, it only took Him days. And He is the same one who gives you strength and faith for the day, every morning.

The calendar is really an invention of man. We don't have months or years to live, we only have days. We have to live the day, but without forgetting the distant tomorrow. That splendid future that awaits us at the end of this life.

When you learn that, is when you start to live.

- It would be interesting to celebrate "birthday-days" instead of birthdays, said young Roberto.

-Yes, Henry replied, smiling, -it could for example be celebrated every 400 days.

We can imagine a meeting between two families saying: "Hi, your baby is so cute, how old is he, he has just turned 400 days old.

And yours? Mine is older, he's 600 days old and he's already walking. I am his mother and I recently turned 8000 days old (20 years).

 And how old are you? 8,800 days. Ah, how nice! This is Grandma, she is 24000 days (60 years old)".

- Ha how funny! -exclaimed Roberto

-Yes, and much more real," added Henry still laughing.

-How about if we go horseback riding tomorrow and you show me around.?

-Yes, said Roberto, -we can go and see a beautiful waterfall called "El Salto del Indio" that very few people know about.

- Fantastic! said Henry,

-But first I want to ask you a favor. Could you please take my friend's car to the city and leave it in the supermarket parking lot? Please leave the keys in the glove compartment and call this number and say that the car is ready to pick it up. I will pay you extra.

- Okay, all right! - said Roberto enthusiastically. -

I'll pick you up early tomorrow morning then? -

- Yes, of course! I'll be expecting you tomorrow, said Henry finally.

Monica's Decision

She got the message and went to get her car from the supermarket. She found the keys and a little note from Henry that read:

Dear Monica,

My heart beats and misses you. It beats and misses you again. It races when I think that we are going to meet.

But then I think that I can't ask you to come with me It's too risky and you have too much to loose.

However, the love I feel for you doesn't let me reason and I dream... I dream that we live together and we are happy. You me and Mike... I love you too much!

Love, Henry

PS: Let some time pass, come see me and we'll talk about it.

A few tears escaped her and then she stood still for a long time, looking out the window of her car. Suddenly she realized what a momentous decision she had to make and the implications it would have on her life and that of her son. Her job, Mike's studies, her home, her friends, her city... She couldn't think clearly.

She went into the supermarket to buy a few things and tried to concentrate.

When she got home and while eating she read the note to Mike. This time it was Mike's eyes filled with tears.

His mother hugged him and Mike said:

-Don't worry about me, I have only 3 weeks of classes left and I am free. Next year I can study in any other school.

This time it was Monica's time to cry. Her chest was burning with longing to be with Henry, but her mind was giving her all kinds of reasons not to venture into something like that.

She had been alone for several years now, even though she had a good job. Her son was in a good school and lived in a good house. Her life revolved around her son. However, he needed a father figure. She also needed a companion and she felt she had found one. She had fallen in love with Henry.

That night before going to sleep, she knelt down and asked God for wisdom and understanding to know how to decide and to be clear about what to do.

She received this answer: "Do it without fear and stay calm and at peace". Thank you Lord," she exclaimed, happy to know what she had to do.

After 30 days, a prudent time to calm things down, she went with Mike to the cabin in the mountain range.

The reunion was beautiful, joyful and full of tenderness. Together they enjoyed a few wonderful days, riding horses or walking, knowing the undulating roads surrounded by native trees, wild flowers and breathing the aroma of the forests of the pre-mountain range.

Roberto, who always accompanied them, became their friend and guide. He had left behind his pessimism and felt encouraged and happy.
Having new friends who appreciated him gave him a new perspective and a new zest for life.
 He learned to enjoy life, to see with different eyes the blue sky, the green of the meadows and to feel the clean air filling his lungs.

A Glimpse into the Future

One evening while they were eating on the terrace, Henry, Monica, Mike, and Roberto were watching the sunset. Mike asked Henry what would happen if the discovery he had made fell into the hands of the powerful, of those who rule the world?

-Today, Henry began, there are pages on the Internet like http://calcular.onlinegratis.tv/dias-vividos/ , where we can know the exact days, months, minutes and even seconds that a person has lived up to the present day. But of course, they can't calculate what is left to live, since they don't have the secret number of each one, which I have discovered.

-Well, let's do a little science fiction, said Henry.

-Let's imagine that I am captured by your agents and "voluntarily" taken to the United States and placed in a technology testing laboratory.

  There I am connected to state-of-the-art 4K cameras with hundreds of megapixels observing my iris, while I dictate the numbers I see.

Perhaps with the help of nanotechnology and microchip they could establish a computer model, a program that establishes the coincidence between the colors, tonalities and numbers that I can see.

They could create software capable of reading, as I do, the numbers hidden behind the iris on a person.

At first it would be tested on a small scale on people who are about to die or are very close to death. Then once perfected, the program would be tested on a large scale and marketed to governments of various countries in order to establish "public policy" on the population of the planet.

Eventually the program would be sold to private entities such as Clinics, Foundations, Financial Entities, Insurance Companies, etc.

In addition, entire families could take advantage of the benefits of this program that we can call "Term of Life" known by its acronym in English TOL (Term of Life) where everyone gets to know the benefits of the program.

That means exactly how many days he or she has left to live. This program is implemented for children as young as 10 years old.

Mainly large and wealthy families use this TOL program to create a strategy to achieve goals, with clear objectives and priorities in their companies, taking into account the time of life of each member of the family.

The entities, companies and consortiums that have this program could select their labor mass according to this important personal data of each one.

A financial institution such as a bank or an insurance company would select with absolute certainty to whom to sell or not to sell a life insurance policy or a mortgage loan or a loan.

In short, the powerful would have a lethal weapon to control the inhabitants of the planet.

Today it is said that the new oil of the world is data, information, which allows whoever has it, a powerful control of people.

We must realize that what I have discovered is very valuable insider information that they would have.

Can you imagine that an optical reader, in an airport or in any other place where people pass through, knows everything about you, where you live, what you buy, etc. and also how many days you have left to live. It would be terrible.

I would not like such a scary world and I am not at all willing to be part of such a controlled future. Henry finished saying.

The Combat

One day, Roberto took them to visit an indigenous Mapuche reserve, the community was on the banks of the Biobío River. It had about 20 rucas arranged in a semicircle. From there we could appreciate the river and its crystalline waters, together with abundant vegetation. The waterfall of sparkling water fell from the top of the rock, "Salto del Indio" (the Indian's jump).

Although they received tourists from time to time, these were not very frequent at that time of the year.

Roberto introduced them to the Lonco, (The Lonco Mapuche is the great Indian chief). a strong man with black eyes and a deep gaze, about 70 years old. He offered them an infusion of yerba mate that was shared among all of them, the Lonco and the Machi, (The Machi is the woman sorcerer of the Mapuches), together with Roberto, Monica, Henry and also Mike.

- What a beautiful place to live! - Monica exclaimed.

-You can stay as long as you want. - Said the Lonco.

-We have a special house for visitors. Besides, you can help us. Roberto told us that you, Mr. Henry, have a very particular gift.

-What can we do for you? said Henry, kindly.

-Look, he said, our community is being decimated by a strange disease that is killing everyone over the age of 50. Near that age they start to get sick and end up dying hopelessly. A team of doctors have come and have not yet discovered what it is. The machi, my brother and I are the only ones over 50 who have not been attacked by this disease.

- Could you help us? the Lonco finished.

Henry hesitated for a moment, looking at Monica. She looked back at him with tenderness and enthusiasm.

- Well, she finally said, -we'll see what we can do. I can't promise anything, but we will do our best.

The machi, who had not spoken until that moment, said:

- The spirits of the water, the wind and the trees, have whispered your arrival, so you are welcome. We will prepare a toasted flour soup for you, while my assistant Antu, takes you to your dwelling.

Monica and Henry were given a special ruca for themselves. Roberto and Mike another one, both by the river.

They could clearly hear the singing of the water and the chirping of the birds that at that hour were getting ready to sleep. The pure air smelled of a soft perfume of laurel flowers, while the falling sun painted everything reddish, leaving the foam of the waterfall whiter and orange.

That night they shared with the entire indigenous community, mostly young people and small children. There was a welcoming dance and Henry was presented to everyone as a visiting Machi, sent by Neguechen, the higher spirit worshipped by the Mapuche.

Henry was a little nervous, while Monica, always positive, squeezing his hand whispered; everything will be fine.

That night, Monica asked God for wisdom and guidance and to guide Henry in the search for the evil that afflicted the community. Henry, who listened, was in total agreement with that request, as he felt the enormous responsibility that was falling on him.

The next day, he asked the Lonco to examine all the members of the community, starting with the children over 10 years old, men and women. There were only 6 people over 50, including the Lonco and the Machi.

Only one of them, called Aukan, caught Henry´s attention when he saw that he had only a few days left to live. Although he looked strong and healthy, the number Henry saw in his iris was very low. He was about to turn 50 and he asked him if he was expecting any special gifts for his birthday.

. -Nothing special. Just a big party with lots of "Muday," he said with a laugh.

Talking to Monica afterwards he said, -this man can give us the key to what is going on.

- Yes, said Monica, - but are these the only elders?

-No, said the Lonco. -There is also Raiquen, my younger brother, who lives a little out of the way. From here you can see his ruca. This afternoon he will come to talk with us.

His younger brother, about 60 years old, is suspicious and does not want Henry to examine him. The Lonco reassures him that it is a simple eye exam. He finally agrees and Henry discovers that this man will live as long as Aukan, the Indian who will have his birthday in a few days.

- They will both die on the same day! - I whisper quietly to Monica. She kept silent in surprise.

On the day of Aukan's birthday party, a table is prepared with all kinds of food, everyone dresses in colorful costumes and begins to dance the "Choique Purun" or "Ostrich dance" to the rhythm of the Kultrún and the Trutruca (Mapuche instruments). There is joy, smiles and a lot of Muday to drink.

The Lonco, using a beautiful colorful costume adorned with colorful tattoos, calls for Aukan, the celebrated one, who bows before him.

-You will be the one to take command of this tribe when I am no longer here-declared the Lonco

- No! - shouts Raiquen, the younger brother of the Lonco.

- This man has refused to drink the potion that the Machi has prepared for his birthday!

- The Lonco, looking at Aukan, asks - is this true?

-Yes, Aukan answers. -That potion is poisoned!

Shouts of astonishment are heard in the community.

-Silence! shouts the Lonco. - Bring that potion here.

The Machi approaches with the concoction in her hands.

Raiquen, the brother of the Lonco, interposes himself in front of her and with a spear in his hand says:

- I challenge to death Aukan who is a coward!

- I accept! shouts Aukan immediately,

-But first I want you to know that Raiquen is guilty of the deaths in this community and the Machi is his accomplice, said Aukan.

The Machi, finding herself discovered, in an abrupt manner threw the clay fountain, spilling all its contents to the ground.

Silence, nobody moves! shouted the Lonco, raising his stone axe.

- The challenge was accepted, make room for the duel to take place. Let your weapons be prepared... And may the God Neguechén decide your end.

Henry, Monica, Mike and Roberto could not believe what was happening. Trying to put a stop to the situation, they addressed to the Lonco, but he was not willing.

With a serious face and attentive eyes, the Lonco waited for the duel to begin. The opponents were ready one in front of the other. In their right hand an axe, in the other a spear. In their belt a dagger.

The Lonco raised his right hand and held it there for a few seconds. A "Queltehue" bird shrill was heard, breaking the silence of the mountain landscape.

As he descended his hand, the dice was cast, the mortal combat began.

Both jumped forward with their axes raised, colliding with a sharp blow without hurting their opponent, falling both tied up and rolling on the ground. As soon as they could, they got up looking for a nearby weapon.

Raiquen grabs his spear a second before Aukan and throws it hard, looking for the heart of his opponent. The latter receives the sharp point, cutting his side. He loses his balance and falls to the ground kicking up the dust of the earth.

With effort he pulls out his knife, but Raiquen rushes at him to finish him off.

Aukan takes the opportunity to bury the dagger in Raiquen's heart, and pushes him to the side.

Both are seriously wounded, but it is Raiquen who faints first and dies. The duel was over.

The women rushed to heal the wounds, to stop the blood that was spilled there. A few hours later, Aukan also died.

The afternoon was already falling, the sun and the mountain peaks were dyed red, the snow painted in a salmon color. The river continued its constant march as if washing the wounds, as if carrying away those memories so that they would not remain stranded in the mind.

With a tired air, the Lonco gave instructions for the burial of both warriors.

The Machi was banished to a distant tribe.

Later, the Lonco, touching Henry's shoulder, said to him:

-This is something that almost never happens... We are a peaceful people. Now everything is all right my friend, everything has been solved.

-I know, I know, said Henry

Monica approached her son to inquire about his condition.

Mike told her:

-Don't worry mom, I'm a grown man.

Then, all saddled their horses, and before it got dark, they started back the way they had come.

After arriving, Monica said:

-What was all this, it was like something out of a movie, it was all so unreal.

- Yes, this was something exceptional, said Henry

-The Araucanos are a peaceful people. However, there is something that calls my attention and leaves me puzzled...

The Enigma Solved

Early the next morning...

- What's the matter Henry? I see you getting more and more serious and quiet, as if something is starting to worry you more and more, commented Monica.

 -I have a growing doubt. There is something that doesn't add up in these numbers. The results in the indigenous community call my attention powerfully. Since I read these numbers in the iris, the same number is being repeated many times. So I need to do a study of young people, or better yet, children no older than 10 years old. We must get a group of them to study them, explained Henry.

- I have a friend! exclaimed Monica -She's a rural school principal. I think I can get her to help us. I'll call her.

- Perfect! replied Henry enthusiastically.

On Monday they arrived at the Escuela Básica Coyanco, in the Bíobío region.

There, they met a group of fifth graders, most of them with Mapuche surnames, who lived nearby. They were all around 10 years old and Henry was going to examin their eyes.

It was an entertaining and instructive activity for them.

First Henry gave a talk to the children about the eye, the iris and Iriology. Then he proceeded with the exams on each one.

He examined 32 children and each one had almost identical numbers: 12867, with a variation of a few days depending on the date of birth of each one.

Monica left each child with a little gift; a small, colorful planner.

 Back at the cabin, Henry analyzed the results of the study.

He was completely surprised; how could almost the same number be repeated in different individuals?

And even more so when he realized how little time 10-year-old children had left to live.

The figure he read for each child was 10220 days with very little variation from one child to the next. If we subtract from this the 10 years lived, that is 3659 days, they have only 6561 days left, equivalent to only 18 more years.

Monica exclaimed, -18 years is the same as you found on Mike!

- Yes, it is very strange! - replied Henry.

We are at the end of 2019 and in 18 more years we will be in 2038. Why does the figure only go that far?

- Well, said Monica, -that's the way the world is going, climate change, ocean pollution....

Exactly! - shouted Henry,

 -That's it, now I understand why!

- His eyes filled with tears. Henry was thrilled.

-What's wrong my love? said Monica.

- Now I understand why! said Henry. What an amazing discovery!

 -Now I understand why the number behind the iris has been revealed to us in such a time!

-It is because the world must know it!

-That is the message: We have no more time left!

All the young people, children and of course the elderly that I have examined their eyes, will not live beyond 2038!

- I haven't found a single person past that date! I don't know how I didn't see it before!

- The world is sick and it only goes until that date, there is no more time!

We don't know the day nor the hour, only the year: 2038!

For all of us, the most we have left to live is 18 years!

- The year 2038 is the end of the world!

Note: "The end of the world" is understood by the vast mayority of cristians, as the second coming of Jesus Christ. Who wil come with great power and glory on the clouds of heaven. For as lightning that comes from the east is visible even in the west, so will be the coming of the Son of Man. The sun will be darkened and the moon will not give its light. (Mt 24)

Before this great day of the end, a world ruler must rise to world power (2 Thess 2:1-4). The Bible indicates that this world leader called the antichrist, will rule the world for 7 years. (Dan 9: 27th).

So, if Henry's discovery is correct, the antichrist should fully rise to power at the end of the year 2030 and begin his regime in 2031, ending the year 2038. Just when Jesus returns and the rapture takes place and the wrath of God is unleashed. (Matt 24:31)

The Email

Here is the email that Henry sent to the judge.

Dear Mr. Judge,

I am Henry. You gave me a photo of yourself so I could examine your iris, remember?

Well I am sorry to tell you that it was not possible for me to do it through a photo, I have to do it, in situ, personally.

However, at the conclusion of my studies after years of tests with different people I can assure you that you will not live beyond the year 2038.

Not only you, but all the inhabitants of the planet.

Well, as you are 70 years old, it will be unlikely for you to live until that date. However, this is an urgent warning to all the inhabitants of the earth, especially the younger ones.

The world has only eighteen years left to live and they will fly by.

I understand that it will be difficult, for you and for many, to believe such a startling revelation. However, in view of how the world is today in 2019, with global warming, indiscriminate logging of forests, earthquakes, hurricanes, drought, natural disasters, plagues and more and more frequent revolts of the people, it will no longer be so hard to believe that the end is near.

But of course many will scoff, others will not take it seriously. They will say it is a joke and laugh in disbelief.

Others will surely call me crazy, and will scorn and discredit this notice.

However, it is my duty to tell you. Whether you believe it or not, is up to you. You have been warned!

However, I would also like to remind you that this world is not our final home. We are going to a better place where there are no crosses on the ground, where there is no crying and no more sadness. Only what lives, only what grows... where we will live forever.

Sincerely, Henry

The End

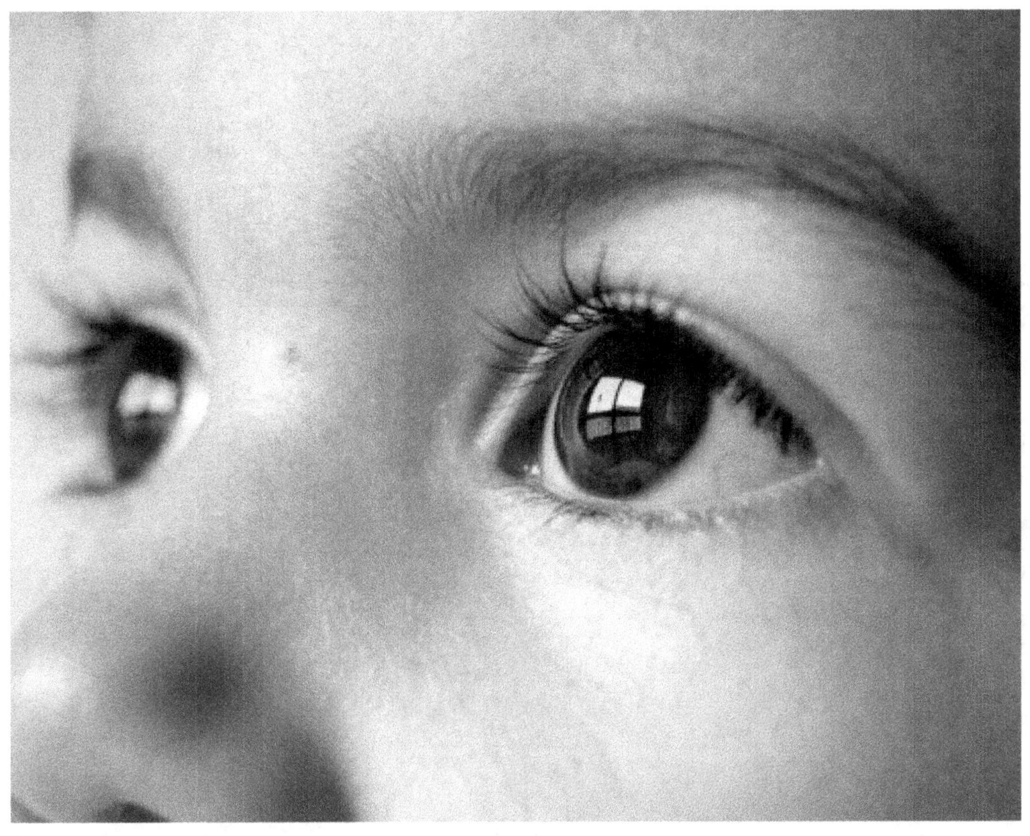

These pure eyes of the Mapuche children have revealed it!